What's So Big About Cleveland, Ohio?

by Sara Holbrook

Illustrated by Ennis McNulty

Gray & Company, Publishers

Cleveland

To my friend, Bob . . .
for listening.
— S.H. —

Gray & Company, Publishers
1588 East 40th Street Cleveland, Ohio 44103
(216) 431-2665
www.grayco.com

Printed in the United States of America

Library of Congress Cataloging-in-Publication Data
Holbrook, Sara.
What's so big about Cleveland, Ohio? /
by Sara Holbrook; illustrations by Ennis McNulty.
[1. Cleveland (Ohio)—Fiction.]
I. McNulty, Ennis, ill.
II. Title.
PZ7.H6957Wh 1997
[Fic]–dc21   97-33914

ISBN 1-886228-02-7

First Edition

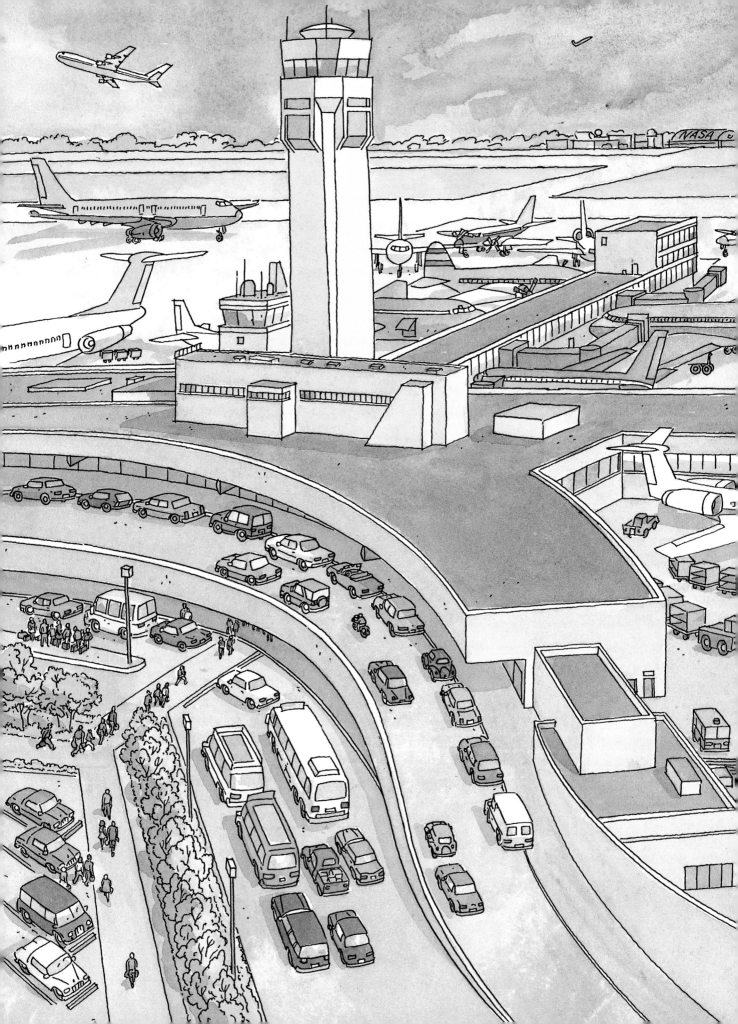

Usually Alan could get pretty excited about a trip to Cleveland Hopkins Airport. He liked to stand in the parking lot, where the departing planes made his hair stand straight up.

He liked to ride back and forth on the people-movers.

He liked to ride up and down on the escalators.

But not today.

Today Amanda arrived.

Alan knew Amanda, and he knew she never just came for a visit. Amanda was like an invasion—she came, she saw, she complained.

Amanda had been around the world about fifteen times. Probably more. Her parents were photojournalists and they took her everywhere—places Alan wasn't even sure how to spell.

Alan knew Amanda, and he knew what to expect.

Amanda would be bored.

Everything bored Amanda.

Alan remembered how Amanda sighed when she was bored.

Alan remembered how Amanda rolled her eyes when she was bored.

And Alan remembered that nothing bored Amanda more than Cleveland, Ohio.

Alan's mom and Amanda's mom had been best friends since they were age zero. They just assumed that Alan and Amanda would be friends, too. Alan's mom even made him cancel his plans for the whole week so he could spend every day with Amanda-the-bored.

"After all," she had told him, "Amanda moves around so much she doesn't have many friends."

Big surprise, thought Alan. (Alan's mother never had to share the back seat of a car with Amanda.)

Alan remembered Amanda was like having a crooked eyelash and a blister at the same time. She was annoying from head to foot.

When the plane arrived and spilled its passengers into the airport waiting area, Alan avoided the hugging and squealing by standing far away with his arms crossed, watching.

They piled the suitcases into the car and started home to Alan's house. The mothers talked and laughed together in the front seat.

In the back, Amanda said, "This airport isn't very big at all. It's so puny I'm surprised the pilot could even find it. Boy, what a boring place to land."

Great, thought Alan as he sank deep and deeper into his seat.

At home, as they were unloading the car, Alan's friend Ramón rode by on his bike calling, "Hola, Alan."

"Hola amigo," Alan returned his wave.

"Hasta la vista." "That's 'See you later' in Spanish," Alan explained to Amanda.

"What's so big about that?" said Amanda. "Last year I learned Swahili. I bet no one around here knows that."

She turned her back, hoisted a bag over her shoulder, and strode proudly inside.

"Swahili! Where do they speak Swahili?" Alan shook his head. One thing Alan did know: in any language Amanda was a drag.

At that moment, the upcoming week yawned before him

like a wide-open mouth full of food.

"Disgusting," thought Alan.

Alan sat himself down with hunched shoulders and a lot of lip. He thought about his choices. He could just grit his teeth and ignore her all week. But then Amanda would leave still thinking she was the World-Wide Queen of Bigger and Better.

OR, maybe, just maybe, he could prove to Amanda that there really was something *even* bigger and *even* better right here in Cleveland, Ohio.

"I'll show her," said Alan to the bushes. And he nodded and stood, put his hands on his hips, and marched inside,

determined.

On Monday morning, Alan and Amanda and their mothers went downtown to the Terminal Tower to watch the incredible leaping fountain and to shop in Tower City.

"Look at that!" said Alan, pointing to the arcs of water that were just then jumping all at once.

"What's so big about that?" asked Amanda. "I've been to the Eiffel Tower in Paris, France—it's very famous. The fountains there are big enough to swim in. "And," she sniffed, "the shops in Paris are *très élégant.*"

Alan decided that being with Amanda was like having a raspberry seed stuck in your teeth. Pretty annoying.

Next they walked down to the Flats, where the Cuyahoga River meets Lake Erie.
"There must be a *bazillion* sea gulls," said Alan.

The sea gulls squawked and scattered on the wind like confetti. The sky was
Superman blue and Lake Erie reflected it like a bright mirror.

"What's so big about that?" said Amanda. She explained that she had been to
the Mediterranean Sea, where she was sure the color blue had been invented.

All kinds of boats were busy entering and leaving the river—speed boats, sail
boats, even a huge ore boat. "See the one with the pointed bow?" said Alan. "That's
a 'salty'. It's headed up to the St. Lawrence Seaway and out to the Atlantic Ocean."

"Big deal," said Amanda. "Hong Kong is the biggest port in the whole wide
world. Or maybe . . ." she hesitated dramatically, "Maybe it's Rotterdam. Hmmm."
She thought it over. "Anyway," she shrugged. "I've been to both of them.
Twice. Much bigger than this."

A bazillion sea gulls squawking at once weren't half as annoying as **a single squawk out of Amanda.**

On Tuesday they went to the Cleveland Metroparks Zoo, where Alan showed Amanda the giant elephants and wild cats, monkeys, and giraffes.

"Boring," proclaimed Amanda.

"In Kenya there's this wildlife preserve where the animals get to run around free and all the people who visit ride around in cages on wheels."

"But wait 'til you see the best part," said Alan excitedly, bouncing and leading everyone toward the rainforest exhibit. "It has indoor rain storms—with thunder and lightning!"

Inside, Amanda was not impressed. "This is nothing compared to the real rainforests in Brazil. In a real rainforest the plants are so big they can eat a kid alive—if she isn't fast on her toes."

Amanda said she was always fast on her toes.

Too bad, thought Alan.

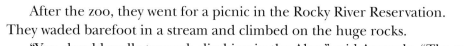

After the zoo, they went for a picnic in the Rocky River Reservation. They waded barefoot in a stream and climbed on the huge rocks.

"You should really try rock climbing in the Alps," said Amanda. "The tallest ones are in Switzerland," she added. "Those mountains are so high they have snow all year 'round and the tops disappear into the clouds."

Later, as they were packing up their picnic, it began to rain. Alan ran for the car, but Amanda just strolled and shouted after him, "This rain is wimpy. I was in a hurricane in Hawaii once and the raindrops were the size of basketballs. *That* was some big rain," she said, impressed with herself.

Amanda was more annoying than rain-soaked shoes
that slosh when you walk and pull your socks down.

What a drip, thought Alan.

Early Wednesday morning they went to the West Side Market, where the moms bought at least forty-seven bags full of fresh fruits and vegetables. Alan ended up carrying most of the bags, because Amanda's hands were busy describing the

big, big, big markets she had seen in Marrakesh, Morocco.

Alan didn't like raw onions. They left a nasty taste in your mouth for hours.

But Alan was pretty sure the nasty taste Amanda left would last all summer.

Amanda was worse than raw onions.

Later, they took the Rapid downtown and had lunch with Alan's father at the old Arcade. "Did Alan tell you that this is one of the oldest covered shopping centers in the U.S.?" asked Alan's dad as he passed out ice cream cones.

Amanda turned and muttered to Alan, "You call this old? The pyramids of Egypt are old. The Great Wall of China is old. This place is only about one minute old compared to them."

Alan looked to his dad for help, but he was busy talking and pointing out flags.

How come nobody else noticed how annoying Amanda was? Even chicken pox gets passed around so other people can appreciate how miserable it makes you. It didn't seem fair that Alan had to endure Amanda all by himself.

Riding home on the Rapid, Amanda said, "If this was a Japanese bullet train, we'd be home by now."

Alan just stared at her.

"Fast," she said.

"Much faster than this."

Once Alan got a mouthful of hot chili. It burned up his insides and made him want to spit across the room. Amanda was a lot like hot chili.

On Thursday, they visited the Natural History Museum in University Circle. Alan was certain Amanda would be impressed by its dinosaurs and planetarium.

"The Smithsonian Museum in Washington, D.C. is way bigger than this," announced Amanda with her hands on her hips.

She was sure it had more dinosaurs, too. And probably more stars in the planetarium.

Alan wondered why something as cool as a dinosaur would become extinct— and something like Amanda would be left to live and breathe.

Weird.

Next they took a walk through Wade Park and strolled around the lagoon toward Severance Hall.

"Alan's school takes a field trip here each year to hear the Cleveland Orchestra," said Alan's mom. "Too bad they're not performing today."

"Yeah, too bad," Alan said. "They're world famous."

"Too bad you didn't get to see them in Tokyo," Amanda quickly responded. "I got to hear a concert *and* shake hands with the Emperor."

That night they went to crowded Jacobs Field to watch the Cleveland Indians play (and to pig out on popcorn).

But as soon as they found their seats, Amanda let out a big sigh.

"Baseball is *sooo* boring."

Amanda said that when it came to sports, she really preferred the bullfights in Mexico City.

"Bullfights are much more exciting than plain old baseball. And of course, the stadiums are a whole lot bigger," she said.

She liked the popcorn, though. She ate Alan's share.

Before this visit, Alan thought the only bad thing about summer was mosquitoes. Amanda was much more annoying than a mosquito.

On the way home, they drove past the Rock & Roll Hall of Fame, which Amanda *almost* thought was cool—until she remembered that she'd been to Memphis, Tennessee, home of the King of Rock and Roll himself. "I saw Elvis Presley's bathroom in Graceland," she bragged. "That was cool."

Alan rode home in silence, just staring at the sky.
Alan said nothing.
Amanda said,

"The sky really *is* bigger in Montana, you know."

On Friday they visited Alan's favorite place.
Alan liked the zoo.
      Alan liked dinosaurs.
         Alan liked baseball. A lot.
            But Alan *loved* to visit the NASA Lewis Space Center.
That was until he heard that Amanda had been to Space Camp.

Alan got poison ivy once and had to paint his legs with pink lotion.

Alan wished there was a pink lotion
            to paint on Amanda.

By that afternoon, Alan was no longer determined to impress Amanda. He didn't even talk to her. When Alan's mother asked why he was so quiet, Alan said he had lost his voice. She reminded him that Amanda was leaving tomorrow and that she was sure he would find his voice soon.

When Alan still wasn't talking at dinner, his mother just said,

"Aaaallllaaaannn . . ."

in that patient voice that meant she was losing her patience.

Alan was trying extra-hard not to tell Amanda exactly how annoying she was. He was afraid she would tell him she'd once met someone even more annoying—in Alaska or Australia.

One thing Alan knew for sure, Amanda was definitely the most annoying person in Cleveland, Ohio.

After dinner, Ramón and some of Alan's other friends came over to play kick-the-can in Alan's back yard.

Then, Alan *did* talk to Amanda. But *only* to ask her to play and *only* because his mother said he had to.

"You'll probably think kick-the-can is really boring," said Alan. "So you might as well not play."

"I probably *will* think it's boring," said Amanda. "But I guess I will play," she sighed and rolled her eyes. "Nothing could be more boring than just sitting around in Cleveland, Ohio."

Ramón explained the rules of kick-the-can to Amanda, because she had never played. She was a fast learner.

Amanda hid.

Amanda ran.

Amanda yelled, **"Kick the can!"** when she was first to reach the goal.

"I WIN! I WIN!"

When it was time to come in, everyone said goodbye to Amanda like she was a person instead of a mosquito, which Alan found particularly annoying.

And then, while Amanda and Alan were having a snack before bed, Amanda suddenly announced,

"I think this place is the greatest!"

Alan choked so hard his juice almost ran out his nose.

"What?" he gagged.

"I mean it," said Amanda. "You have grass, you have trees. You have ten thousand places to hide. You have all kinds of cool friends," she said sincerely. "You have the best backyard in the whole world."

Alan looked out the window and he looked at Amanda.

"I guess you're right," he said.

"Of course I am," said Amanda.

The fact that Amanda could be annoying even when she was saying something nice was no surprise to Alan. But he felt better anyway.

"When I come back next year, do you think we can play kick-the-can?" asked Amanda.

Alan sighed and rolled his eyes. "I guess so," he answered. Then he smiled a winning little smile. At last he knew something that Amanda couldn't know. After all, Amanda didn't live in Cleveland, Ohio.

"Of course, if you come in the summer again you'll miss the *best* game in the whole wide world."

"WHAT!" said Amanda in a word that sounded a little disgusted, a little discouraged and very annoyed all at once.

"Yeah," Alan said knowingly as he popped a grape into his mouth and stood up to leave. "In the fall it gets dark early."

"WHAT'S SO BIG ABOUT THAT?"
demanded Amanda.

Alan smiled a big, big smile.